DISCLAIMER!

This is a work of fiction. Unless otherwise indicated, all the names, characters, businesses, places, events, and incidents in this book are either the product of the author's imagination or used in a fictitious manner. Any resemblance to actual persons, living or dead, or actual events is purely coincidental.

Volume One: Wren's First Battle

1

Saturday morning, her alarm clock from her pink iPhone with a My Melody phone case on it woke her up. "Ugh!" She groaned, hitting her phone that's next to her pillow. She pressed the stop button on her alarm and walked to the bathroom to get dressed for swim practice.

Her name was Wren Sky. She was a African-American 19 year old self-published author, a swimmer and a college student for dental hygienist. She was not on the swim team right now. The swim practice she practiced at was the Athletic Center. They don't have a swim team. They have a training group. Wren moved up to the advanced stage. She had been going there ever since she was in high school. She lived at home with her twin sister named Mikayla and a loving mother and a father named Tina Sky and Joseph Sky. She had an older brother, but he's living on campus. She was the oldest twin for 2 minutes, but the shortest in the family. Her height was 4'11 and Mikayla's height was 5'2. People assumed Mikayla is the oldest because she's taller than Wren.

In the bathroom, she put her light blue swimsuit under her pink hoodie and blue jean skirt with black biker shorts and put her hair in a high ponytail.

She walked out of the bathroom and packed her swim bag. "Are you ready, Wren?" Mikayla asked, poking her head out of the bedroom door. "Yes, I just need to fill up my water bottle. Can you fill it up for me, please?" she asked Mikayla, holding out her green Gatorade water bottle. "Sure," she agreed and took the water bottle to the kitchen. Wren zipped her pink swim bag and followed Mikayla downstairs.

In the kitchen, Mikayla filled Wren's water bottle and gave it to her in the living room. "Thanks, sis," Wren smiled while sitting on the couch. "You're welcome. Sorry that your car is in the shop. At least we're picking it up tomorrow." "It's fine, I'm glad you, mom, and dad get to see me swim on my last day before the next training season. I wish I could join a swim team but I can't find one," she cried. Mikayla sat next to her and petted her head. "Don't worry, Wren. You'll find a team someday. Just appreciate the training group. They're helping you relieve your stress and anxiety." "I know, but it's not the same though. I want to join a swim team to have fun, compete, and make a whole bunch of friends who are competitive and love to swim like me." "Well, let's see what the future holds."

After their conversation, their parents, Tina and Joseph walked down the stairs with their jackets and shoes on. Mrs.Sky was wearing a dark blue jacket and Mr.Sky was wearing a gray jacket. "Are you ready to go, Sport?" Mr.Sky happily asked. "Yeah, I guess," Wren sadly sighed. "What's wrong?" Mrs.Sky worried. "I've been training at the Athletic Center for years. And I noticed I haven't joined a team yet. I wish I could join a team," she cried, grabbing her swim bag and walking towards her mom and dad. Mr.Sky rubbed her head and gave her a smile. "Don't worry, Sport. You'll join a team. Maybe we can help you look for one after practice since it's your last day." "Sure, we can do that," Wren happily agreed and walked to her mom's red family van. Mr. and Mrs. Sky and Mikayla followed her.

Ten minutes later, they arrived at the Athletic Center. They walked into the building and the pool area. Wren changed into her swimsuit and her parents and Mikayla sat at a white table that was six feet away from the lap pool Wren practiced at. Wren exited the women's locker room and entered the pool, waiting for her coach and the rest of her classmates. In the meantime, she practiced freestyle, backstroke, butterfly, breaststroke and mermaid kicks. Mermaid kicks were her favorite.

Twenty minutes later, Wren's coach and three of her classmates entered the pool and the coach started practice.

Her coach's name was Coach Samuel. He had freckles all over his body and face. He had blonde hair under his black swim cap. The classmates were much older than Wren. All of them were still in the beginner stage. Whenever they struggle, Wren was always there to help. With her help, she made her classmates feel confident and brave.

"Good Morning, swimmers," Coach Samuel greeted, clapping his hand, waking everyone up. Except Wren. She was filled with energy. "Good Morning, Coach Samuel," they all greeted back. "For our last day of class before our next training session," he continued. "I'm gonna test all of you." "TEST US?!" they panicked. "Test them?" Mikayla muttered. "EXACTLY!" he smiled. "Today's test is to see how long you can swim using each style without taking a break. 100 yd freestyle, backstroke, breaststroke, and butterfly. The first three people who make it and do it right will get a medal. The fourth person will get a handshake. Get into your starting positions."

Everybody splitted into their own lanes and prepared their freestyle position. "On your mark. Get set. GO!" Coach Samuel blew his whistle and everybody started swimming, using freestyle. "GO WREN! WE LOVE

YOU!" her parents and Mikayla screamed, waving their hands in the air, causing Coach Samuel to chuckle.

During the swim test, Wren was beating everyone. She swam to the end of the wall and went back to the beginning, still doing freestyle. Two other students, a boy and a girl, tried catching up to her, but they were feeling tired. The fourth girl took her time swimming. "If I can't win. That's fine. I'm only doing this to get out of the house from my ten baby siblings. Especially the troublemaking one," she sighed.

Wren swam back to the beginning, did a flip turn, and backstroke back to the exit. "Damn, that girl is fast," the boy commented. "Exactly. Why is she even here? Isn't she supposed to be on a swim team by now?" The girl questioned. Coach Samuel blew his whistle at the boy and the girl. "Less talking and more swimming." "Sorry, sir," They apologized and swam backstroke to the end with Wren.

After Coach Samuel heard their conversation, he looked at Wren, who is swimming faster than the rest of her teammates. "They're right. She swims really fast, but she's not a team yet. Let's see what I can do."

He looked at the black-haired female lifeguard and shouted, "CAN YOU WATCH THEM RACE, PLEASE?! I NEED TO DO SOMETHING REAL QUICK!" The female lifeguard gave him a thumbs up and he walked to his office, typing on his computer.

Fifthteen minutes later, the race was over. Wren was placed in first, the boy who commented on her was placed in second place. The girl who also commented on Wren placed third place. The other girl who has ten siblings is placed in fourth place.

The female lifeguard grabbed Wren's wrist and held her arm in the air screaming, "WREN IS THE WINNER!" "YAY! I WON! I WON!" she cheered, sounding like Chun-Li from *Street Fighter*. Her parents and Mikayla clapped their hands and cheered her on. "CONGRATULATIONS, WREN!" Her swimmates also clapped for her.

Coach Samuel ran out of his office and wrapped a gold medal around Wren's neck. And gave the boy and the girl a silver and bronze medal. And as he promised, he gave the ten sibling girl a handshake.

After awarding them, he looked at the clock and smiled at them. "We have twenty-five minutes left of class. To celebrate, you all can have free time." "YAY!" they all screamed and started swimming all over the pool. Coach Samuel walked towards Wren's parents and sister and asked them, "May we talk in the office, please? I have a surprise for Wren." "Sure. Why not?" Mrs.Sky agreed and they followed him to his office. They sat in front of his brown desk and Coach Samuel sat behind his desk with a MacBook.

"You all noticed I've been training your daughter for four years." "Yes, we did notice that," Mr.Sky nodded his head. "Well, I'm deciding to let her go." "WHAT?!" They panicked. "It's not like I'm banning her. I'm saying I have a team for her that she can participate in," Coach Samuel sweated, thinking her family was gonna gut him. "We're listening," Mrs.Sky calmed down. "The team Wren is going to love to participate in is an adult swim team called *The*

SwordFish Team." "SwordFish Team?" Mikayla questioned. "What do they do?" "I'm glad you asked. It's a travel team. They travel every month to compete and go on field trips. Every spring, they enter the nationals. Your daughter is gonna enjoy this team. She'll be wearing a team jacket, she'll make lots of friends, traveling, partying, and competing. What do you all think?"

Mikayla rubbed her chin with her right hand, feeling nervous. "Kind offer, but I think we rather let her stay here for an extra-" "She'll be happy to take the offer," Mrs.Sky interrupted Mikayla and accepted the offer. "Then it's a deal. Thank you for agreeing. She will do great. Trust me," Coach Samuel cheered, shaking Mrs.Sky's hand. "Do you want me to print the team info for her?" "Yes please," Mr.Sky smiled.

Coach Samuel printed three pages of the swim team info, stapled the pages together, and handed them to Mrs.Sky. "Nice doing business with all of you," he shook Mrs.Sky's hand. "Thanks for everything," Mr.Sky smiled and they all walked out of the office.

Coach Samuel blew his whistle at Wren and the other swimmers and they stopped swimming and stared at him. "You all may be dismissed. See you all, next month."

They got out of the pool and walked to the locker room. Coach Samuel tapped on Wren's shoulder and whispered, "Have fun on your new swim team." "Swim team?" Wren jumped, feeling confused while walking to the locker room.

Wren got out of the locker room and walked to her family. "How was practice?" Mr.Sky asked. "It was good. I won first place on the test. Exercising pays off," she chuckled. "What did your coach say to you?" Mikayla asked, "I saw him whispering to you." "He told me to have fun on my swim team. I wonder what that is about?" Mrs.Sky, Mr.Sky, and Mikayla gave each other the side eye. Mrs.Sky hides the paper behind her back. "What's wrong?" She asked them. "We have a surprise for you," Mr.Sky patted her head. "Surprise?" "Well…technically, the surprise was from your coach," Mrs.Sky corrected

Mr.Sky. "What is it?" "Let's show you in the car," her mom said.

They entered the car and Mrs.Sky gave Wren the swim team papers. "What's with the papers?" she wondered. "Your coach was talking to us in his office about the SwordFish Team. He wants us to see if you're interested in joining the team. He said it's a traveling team and every spring it's nationals season. What do you think? Are you ready?" she responded.

Wren looked through every page and told her mom, "I'm ready." Mikayla began to worry. "Wait a minute. Do you think you should rethink this idea? What happens if you get hurt or injured? Who's gonna help you?" "She'll be fine," Mr.Sky shrugged. "I know she'll do great. She's been more independent ever since she was in middle school." "As soon as we get home, I'm gonna shower and register for the team."

On their way home, Mr.Sky got a phone call from the car shop. "Hello?" He picked up the phone. "Hello sir, your gray Audi will be ready to get picked up tomorrow."

"Okay, thank you for letting me know." And he hung up the phone. "Who was that?" Mrs.Sky asked. "That was the car shop. Wren's car is gonna be ready to get picked up tomorrow." "This day keeps getting better and better," Wren commented, squeezing the papers tightly in her hands.

2

Back at home, Wren was in the bathroom taking a shower. "Ah. This hot water feels great." She got out of the shower, grabbed her towel from the towel hanger that's next to the shower, and wrapped it around her body.

Downstairs in the living room, Mr. and Mrs.Sky were watching TV on the brown couch, while Mikayla was crossing her arms, giving them the death stare. Mr. and Mrs.Sky noticed and turned their heads towards her. "Something wrong, baby?" her mom asked. "Yes, something is wrong," she angrily responded. "Isn't this a bad idea?" "About what?" Mr.Sky questioned. "About Wren joining a swim team. Isn't this scary or something. She has asthma. And what if she gets hurt?" "She's gonna be fine, Mikayla. She's been doing good ever since she's been going to practice," Mrs.Sky said. "Okay, but what happens if she does?" She was worried. "If she gets hurt, then we'll pull her," Mrs.Sky sadly sighed. "Deal," Mikayla agreed, giving her mom a thumbs up. "But it's up to her though," Mr.Sky corrected them. "Okay," Mikayla sighed. Mrs.Sky nodded her head.

Wren walked downstairs with her laptop and sat at the kitchen table, researching the swim team her coach mentioned. Mikayla turned her head around at her, feeling confused. "What are you doing now, Wren?" "I'm browsing on the Swordfish website to see what their team does." "Didn't mom and dad tell you in the car?" "They did, but sometimes there could be more details," she said, typing the team name on Google. "Whatever," Mikayla rolled her eyes and texted her friends on her purple Iphone.

The SwordFish team website had old pictures of their previous competitions, field trips, award ceremony, parties, and new pictures of their pool at a community college. "Isn't it a little cheap to swim at another school's pool?" Wren commented. "Oh well, time to register."

She clicked on the registration page and typed her full name, age, personal info, experiences, favorite strokes, and her goal. "Cool!" She was amazed. "We can type in our goals and strokes."

After registering, she clicked the *enter* button and got a quick email from the coach.

Dear Wren Sky,

Thank you for registering for our SwordFish swim team. We are excited to have a new member like you who will love to compete and have fun. You won't regret making this decision. Before I tell you the first day of practice, let me tell you a lot of things about this team. We are a travel team. We compete twice a month against other teams. Sometimes rematches, but not alot. We don't just compete. We go on field trips and parties. The field trips we have are celebration field trips and vacation trips. The parties we throw are holiday parties like: Halloween and

Christmas. Regular parties we host are BBQ parties, dance parties, skating parties, arcade parties, and more. A new member will get a team shirt and jacket to represent the team. You can wear any swimsuit to practice and swim meets. Once again, thank you for registering. We'll see on September 30th.

Best swim coach,

Coach Nelly.

Wren read the email and smiled full of glee. "Thank you, Coach Nelly," she whispered. She closed her laptop and walked in the living room with her family, standing next to Mikayla. "Did you register?" Mr.Sky asked. "Yes, I did. I start on September 30th." Mikayla checked the calendar on her phone and counted the weeks. "That's in 2 weeks," she checked. "What are you gonna do during those 2 weeks?" "I'm thinking about going shopping tomorrow to buy new gear for practice," Wren replied. "How about your old swim stuff?" Mrs.Sky questioned. "I could use it, but at the same time I can't because I've been using my old swim stuff ever since I went to the Athletic Center and they're falling apart. I'm growing out of my gray swim fins, my black and yellow snorkel is covered with scratch marks, and my swim bag threads are poking out. Do you want to come with me, Mikayla?" "I'm good," she said, folding her arms and crossing her legs like a businesswoman. "You're lost," Wren shrugged and ran to the stairs like Sonic The Hedgehog. "What are you about to do now?" Mikayla wondered. "I'm gonna get my notebook so I can make a list of things to buy for the swim team." She went to her room, grabbed her spiral pink and white polka-dot mini notebook and glitter cat pen and ran back downstairs, sitting next to Mikayla, writing her list.

Things to buy for Swim Team:

- *2 swimsuits (Practice and Competing)*
- *3 pairs of goggles*

- Swim bag
- Swim fins
- Tissue
- Water bottle
- Keychains
- Mini Pouch (Car keys, phone, inhaler)
- SuitCase

She ripped the list out of her notebook and folded it neatly into a small square and put it in her back pocket. "I'll put it in my purse before bed."

Close to midnight, Wren and Mikayla were changing into their pajamas in their bedroom. Wren wore a sky blue undershirt with black shorts and a black hair bonnet on her head. Mikayla wore a purple dress shirt with purple shorts and a purple hair scarf. Purple was her favorite color. Wren turned the bedroom light off and layed in bed. "What do you think of the swim team idea?" she asked Mikayla. "You've been oddly angry and worried.

You don't even have anxiety like me. Is the idea bothering you?"

Mikayla gave out a sad sigh and looked at Wren with puppy eyes. "I'm okay with the swim team idea, but I'm worried that you won't be able to spend time with me." "Huh?" Wren jumped. "Not only that," she continued. "You have asthma and anxiety and I'm afraid you're gonna hurt yourself mentally and emotionally." "That's not true," she corrected her. "Mikayla, I've been practicing at the Athletic Center ever since high school. Whenever I go to practice, I'm not stressed or anxious. Do you wanna know why?" "Why?" "Because swimming relieves my stress. That's not the only reason. Swimming helps me build up so much energy, I workout after practice until I'm out of energy. Swimming and exercising can help with mental health. Thanks to those two things, it helps me stay calm in college, bad days, and bad people. They saved my life." "Wow!" Mikayla was amazed. "I didn't think about it that way." "Starting tomorrow, think about the swim team as an outlet." "I will. Thanks, big sis." "Your welcome," Wren smiled. "And by the way, I will always be here with you. I'll be with you before and after practice." "Yes, Wren. Goodnight." "Goodnight."

The next morning, Wren was in the bathroom, putting her hair in a low ponytail with a left bang sticking out, almost covering her eye. After that, she put medium silver hoop earrings on both of her ears. "Perfect, I'm ready to go." she said. She wore a Cuphead shirt with Cuphead and Mugman on it under her red and black plaid long-sleeve shirt with dark blue jeans.

She went to her bedroom and got her My Melody purse off the floor and went downstairs and put on her black and white sneakers.

Mikayla was downstairs, drawing in her black sketchbook, watching Craig Of The Creek on TV. She turned her head at Wren who was standing by the door. "What are you doing?" she asked. "I'm waiting for dad to wake up so he can take me to the store. My car is still in the shop," she frowned, scratching her head. "Dad already left," Mikayla chuckled, covering her mouth with her black and purple long sleeve sweater. "Where did he go?" Wren asked. "He's at-" ***HONK! HONK!*** Mikayla's answer got interrupted by a car honk coming from outside. "Who's car is that?" she asked. "Let's check it out," Wren suggested.

The twins ran outside and saw Mr.Sky pulling into the house with Wren's car. "Oh my sweet Jesus," Wren's jaw dropped on the porch.

Mr.Sky rolled down the car window and shouted, "Your car is fixed, Wren." "THANKS, DAD!" she screamed and ran to the car. He got out of the car and handed her the keys. "Be careful, sweetheart." "Yes, sir. I will."

Mikayla and Mr.Sky walked inside the house and Wren drove out of the neighborhood. "Time to do some shopping."

3

Wren parked her car in front of the Swim Shop and entered the building, carrying her purse with her shoulder and holding her shopping list in her right hand. "I hope they have everything," she said. "The internet did say this is the best store for swimmers."

Inside the building, there were blue shelves filled with colorful swimsuits, goggles, backpacks, swim fins, kickboards, and books and magazines about swimming. On the ceiling, there were plastic light blue and white seashells dangling all over the store. "Did I die in my sleep? Is this heaven?" She drooled with stars in her eyes. "Let's get to shoppin' cuz this writer is going on a swim team." She grabbed a light blue shopping cart and she ran to the swimsuit aisle.

In the swimsuit aisle, Wren was looking at different kinds of swimsuits. The first section had tie-dye swimsuits. The second section had rainbow colored swimsuits. The third section had swimsuits that are mixed with black red, blue, purple, green, and pink. The fourth, fifth, and sixth sections had camouflage colors for boys and girls. Wren slowly lost interest in the swimsuit designs. "I'll probably check the next aisle," she shrugged, walking to the next aisle.

In the next aisle, There was a giant section filled with Anime swimsuits. My Hero Academia, One Piece, Power Rangers, Miraculous: Ladybug and Cat Noir, Sailor Moon, Attack On Titan, Haikyuu, Free! Swim club, Yuri On Ice, Neon Genesis Evangelion, and Madoka Magica. "Yup! I'm in heaven."

She browsed through every section and saw a white and purple Mirko swimsuit with a yellow moon prism in the middle in the My Hero Academia section. "No way," she smiled, grabbing the small size of the Mirko swimsuit. "They have the swimsuit of my favorite pro-hero. I'll wear this on practice days," she said, putting the swimsuit in her shopping cart. "If I'm wearing an anime swimsuit for practice, maybe I'll get a regular swimsuit for my swim meets." She walked back to the first swimsuit aisle and looked at the swimsuits again. "I'll get this pink and red camouflage swimsuit," she said, taking the swimsuit and putting it in her shopping cart. "Camouflage is my favorite design and pink and red are my favorite colors. Pink is my swimmer side and red is my author side."

She got out of the swimsuit aisle and went to the swim goggle aisle, swim bag aisle, swim fins aisle, and water bottle.

Twenty-five minutes later, Wren was out of breath, panting like a dog. "This is a lot of shopping," she complained, leaning against her cart. "How does Mikayla do this? I love shopping too, but damn. Now I know how my dad feels whenever he goes shopping with my mom."

Wren stood by the cart handle and looked at her stuff. "Alright, let's see what I have in this cart. One anime swimsuit, one camouflage swimsuit, a black, blue, and white clear swim goggles, pink and black swim bag, small dark blue swim fins, and a large teal water bottle. Looks like that's everything from the store. What else do I need to buy?" She pulled her list out of her purse and looked at the items on the list. "Knew it," she sighed. "Looks like I'm going to Target."

She took her cart to self-checkout and checked out all of her stuff. "This is gonna be worth it," she smiled, crying tears of pain because she has to go to another store.

She walked out of the store with her bags and put them in her car trunk. She walked inside of her car and played *Champion* by Carrie Underwood on her phone, connected to the car stereo and drove off to Target.

At Target, she grabbed a shopping cart and headed to the womens' makeup aisle, browsing for a pack of tissues. "Tissues. Tissues. Where are the tissues?"

Wren loved carrying tissues to swim practice because it's very common for swimmers to get water in their noses when they're swimming. Wren's was so bad, if she didn't get the water out of her nose quickly, she would get a nosebleed. She's already used to it.

At the end of the aisle, she found them next to the makeup brushes. "BINGO!" She cheered and put them in her cart. She went to the other makeup aisle and saw a Hello Kitty: My Melody pouch. Her eyes glowed when she saw how clear the pouch was and saw a hot pink zipper attached to it. "I want that," she whispered and put it in her cart. She left the makeup aisle and went to the video game aisle where they have video game keychains.

She browsed at the games first and then browsed at the keychains. "So many keychains," she said. "But there's so much to choose from. I don't want to overfill my swim bag with keychains. I can buy keychains for my swim bag *and* my suitcase. Speaking of which, I need to buy a new one. My old pink one is falling apart. I can probably buy a blue one instead."

Wren grabbed a Sonic, Isabelle from *Animal Crossing,* and Mario keychains for her swim bag. And grabbed Tom Nook from ALSO *Animal Crossing,* a poke-ball, and a Mario red mushroom keychains for her new suitcase. She put them in her shopping cart and walked to the suitcase aisle.

In the suitcase aisle, there were a variety of big suitcases: black, pink, hot pink, sky blue, dark blue, gray, red, yellow, orange, purple, and teal.

Not only the colors, they also had cute designs on them like white polka-dots, black stripes, cheetah prints, and a rainbow one. "I want a design one," Wren jumped out of excitement. "I'll take this sky blue with white polka-dot suitcase. It matches the theme." She took the suitcase off the shelf and put it in her shopping cart. "Finally!" she sighed. "I'm all done. Time to go to the self checkout and go home."

Wren went to self checkout, paid for the items, and took her bags to her car, putting them in the trunk. "Wren Sky, you are ready to shine with the rest of the swimmers," she commented, looking at the sky. "Thank you, God. Thank you for making my dream come true." She went inside of her car and drove back home.

Fifthteen minutes later, Wren entered the house, carrying all her bags. "Hey, family. I'm home." "Do you need help?" Mikayla asked, running towards her. "Sure," Wren agreed and handed the bags to Mikayla. They walked to the living room, and sat the bags down on the floor in front of the brown middle table. Mr.Sky paused the TV and he and Mrs.Sky asked Wren about the bags. "What did you buy for the swim team?" Mrs.Sky asked. Every item Wren held in her hands, she showed and told it to them.

"I bought a Mirko swimsuit, another swimsuit for competitions, swim goggles, new swim fins, new swim bag, and a water bottle from the swim shop." "COOL!" They were all amazed. "What's in the Target bags?" Mikayla kindly asked, peeking through the bags. "I bought a sky blue polka-dot suitcase, six video games keychains for my suitcase and swim bag, and a pack of mini tissues. "Why the tissues? Just wondering," Mr.Sky wondered. "I blow my nose after practice because I get water in my nose all the time. Plus, if I don't get the water out quickly, it will dry out my nose and get me a nosebleed." "That makes sense," he agreed. "Why the suitcase?" Mikayla worried. "The team I'll be in is a travel team. So I want to be super prepared." "Okay, but what happens if you guys have to fly on a plane?" "Then I'll have to conquer my fear and enjoy the fun. Never let fear stop you from having fun." "That was cringy," Mikayla commented, giving herself a facepalm. "Be nice, Mikayla," Mrs.Sky corrected her.

Wren put her stuff back in the bags and carried the bags upstairs. "I'm about to organize my gear and make sure I'm prepared. This team is gonna be very interesting," she smiled, hugging the bags tight.

In the room, Wren put the keychains on her suitcase and put it in the closet, behind the door. While she's in the closet, she hung her new swimsuits next to her gym clothes. To finish the moment, she packed her new swim gear into her new swim bag and added keychains onto it. She kissed her fingers and said, "This is a masterpiece." And put the bag behind the closet door with her suitcase.

"All done," she clapped her hands, jumping up and down. "The only thing I need to do now is wait for the time and go to practice soon." Wren ran back downstairs and chilled with her family.

4

September 30th, 5:15am. Wren's alarm clock on her phone ranged loudly, waking her up. Without a single groan, Wren woke up screaming, "TODAY IS THE DAY!" She stopped her alarm clock and ran to the bathroom to get dressed.

Everytime Wren got excited for an event or a big day, her heart fluttered and shook constantly.

After she brushed her teeth and washed her face, she put her Mirko swimsuit under her red hoodie and jogging pants, put her hair in a high ponytail with a black scrunchie, grabbed her swim bag from the closet, and went downstairs to put her shoes on and grabbed her car keys.

In the kitchen, Wren looked in the pantry for something to eat for breakfast, but there was no more cereal left. She went to the fridge, but there's only whole milk and she's lactose intolerant. "I guess I can get myself some Mcdonald's breakfast after practice," she shrugged, closing the fridge and walking out of the kitchen with her keys in her hand. She walked to her car and drove out of the neighborhood.

Twenty-five minutes later, She arrived at a Livonia building called Athletic Community College (ACC). She got out of the car with her swim bag, looking at the building. "Looks like this is the place." She went inside the building and saw an empty blue and white office with a black computer, a navy blue chair, and papers all over the desk. "Umm…" She felt confused, looking around the office. "Is practice canceled?" "PSSH! PSSH!" whispered a mysterious voice, coming from the door next to the desk. "Who's there?" Wren worried, looking around the room as if there's a ghost haunting the room. "Hey! Come in here," said a mysterious blonde-haired lady with a ponytail, wearing a blue polo shirt that says *SwordFish Team* with a picture of a swordfish on the back of the shirt and jeans, shaking her hand, getting Wren's attention. Wren saw the lady and followed her into the door.

"Are you new here?" the mysterious lady asked, walking Wren to the gym area. "Yes, this is my first time joining this team. My old coach introduced me to this team," Wren explained. "That's great. It's a good thing they showed you. You're gonna love it here. What's your name by the way?" "My name is Wren. Wren Sky," she replied. "Wren Sky," the mysterious lady kindly repeated, "what a cool name. I can tell you're a fast swimmer with a kind, bubbly, and tomboyish personality." "How did you know?" Wren kindly asked. "I can read a swimmer's mind and tell by the looks of a swimmer." "Now that's rad," Wren snapped her fingers.

"Are you my coach?" "Yes I am. I'm sorry if I didn't introduce myself. My name is Nelly Anderson. You can call me Coach Nelly." "Nice to meet you, Coach Nelly. I can't wait to join this team," Wren cheered.

They both entered the gym and Wren saw a bunch of girls sitting down on bleachers with a projector out in front of the white board. "You can sit on the bleachers with the rest of the girls," said Coach Nelly, leading her hand to the bleachers. "Okay," Wren agreed and sat on the bleachers next to a red-haired girl, who was wearing a black shirt with a teal cat face on it and teal leggings.

Coach Nelly stood in front of the white board and started the announcement by blowing her silver whistle, waking the girls up who were nodding their heads to sleep.

"Good morning, ladies. Welcome to our first day of practice. I am your coach, Coach Nelly and we are called THE SWORDFISH TEAM!" she screamed, blowing a red horn in the gym. Few of the girls including Wren got excited, but most of the girls covered their ears because the gymnasium gave the horn a loud echo, causing some of the girls' ears to hurt. "Sorry. Sorry," Coach Nelly apologized. "I forgot the gym and the horn don't go together. Especially in the morning." "It's okay," the girls' said, uncovering their ears.

"Anyway," Coach Nelly continued. "Today we have a new member who joined our team. Her name is Wren Sky and she has a lovely personality. Wren, can you walk up to the board and introduce yourself to the girls, please."

Everyone looked at Wren, who's walking in front of the board, with a big smile on her face. "Hello, everybody. My name is Wren Sky. I'm an author with a pen name called: Sakura Flowers. I have a twin sister and older brother. I'm the oldest twin for 2 minutes. My favorite hobbies are writing, reading, singing, swimming, and exercising. I have been featured in songs with my friend who is a musician and goes by the name BunniBlu. I'm a tomboy with a kind, bubbly personality. Sometimes I can be girly, but I'm mostly a tomboy. I'm in school for Dental Hygiene. Hopefully, I can become a full-time writer one day. I hope I can be friends with all of you." "Any questions for our lovely new member?" Coach Nelly kindly asked, patting Wren's shoulder. Three girls quickly stood up from the bleachers shouting, "YOU'RE SAKURA FLOWERS?!"

The first girl had short black hair with a left bang. She had freckles across her nose and was wearing an orange crop shirt that said _Destiny_ on it with black jogging pants. The second girl was half white and half black with brown poofy hair with a purple bow, wearing a dark and light purple paint shirt and light purple shorts. She had nice shaped curves. The third girl was the red-haired girl who was sitting next to Wren. She looked a little shy.

"You guys read my books?" Wren excitedly asked. "Of course we did," said the first girl, "I bought all of your six volumes of Magical Girl Army and three volumes of the Baseball Princess." "SAME HERE!" screamed the second girl. "WHEN ARE YOU MAKING THE NEXT VOLUME OF MAGICAL GIRL ARMY?!" "I'm still working on it," Wren replied. "Can you post a sneak peek, please?" The third girl quietly asked. "I'm sorry, I can't hear you," Wren kindly commented,"can you speak louder, please?" "Can you post a sneak peek, please?" The third girl repeated her question loudly. "I'll think about it," Wren answered. "I appreciate you all reading my books. After practice, I can give you all my autograph." "DEAL!" They screamed. "COACH!" The first girl yelled. "WE HAVE A FAMOUS AUTHOR ON THE TEAM!" "That is really amazing," Coach

Nelly agreed. "Where can I buy your books at, Wren?"

"You can buy them at Target, Amazon, and my own official website *www.SakuraFlowersBooks.com*." "Great, I'll be sure to read it. Thank you for introducing yourself to us," "You're welcome," Wren smiled and sat back down on the bleachers. "Now we have a new swimmer joining the team. Let's talk more about the team," said Coach Nelly, writing a list of details on the board with a black expo marker.

She put the cap back on the marker and showed the girls the list. "This list I wrote on the board is about the details of this team. Feel free to take a picture of this list."

Wren and the three *fangirls* pulled their phones out of their bags and took a picture of the list on the board. "I'm gonna remember this," Wren whispered to herself.

"About this team," Coach Nelly started the topic, "we are the strongest, fastest, and adventurous travel team in town. We compete twice a month. Few competitions will be in Michigan and out of state. The first swim meets will be medley relays and the second swim meets will be individual relays. Sometimes both. Next week, we'll be preparing for our first battle. Today, we're not swimming." "AW MAN!" Wren and the rest of the girls complained. "Except for Wren," she continued. "Me?" Wren questioned, pointing her index finger at herself. "Yes, ma'am. You. As a new swimmer, you have to challenge me to a 50 yd freestyle race to see how fast you are so I can decide if you're a beginner or advanced." "Uh…" Wren's voice cracks out of fear.

The red-haired *fangirl* put both of her hands on Wren's shoulders, whispering in her ear, "Be careful beating her. She's the fastest swimmer alive. She beated every single one of us and she called us beginners." Wren stood up from the bleachers and pointed her finger at Coach Nelly like Phoenix Wright from Ace Attorney. "I ACCEPT YOUR CHALLENGE!"

Coach Nelly smirked and gave Wren the evil eyes. "Well, then. Follow me." Wren and the rest of the swimmers followed Coach Nelly to the pool area.

Wren and Coach Nelly threw their clothes on the ground with their swimsuits already on from under their clothes. Wren wore her Mirko swimsuit for My Hero Academia and Coach Nelly wore a navy blue swimsuit.

They both stood on the starting blocks, leaning towards the pools with their hands in front of their bodies, placed their right foot in front of the other, curled their toes forward, and grabbed on the edge of the block. "On a count of three, we're gonna start the race," Coach Nelly said. Wren nodded her head with a competitive look on her face. "1…2…3!" They both dove into the pool, swimming freestyle.

The swimmers screamed Coach Nelly's name, but the three *fangirls* screamed Wren's pen name. "GO! SAKURA GO! KICK HER ASS!"

In the pool, Coach Nelly swam faster than Wren, but Wren picked up the paste and beat her at the end of the pool and did a flip turn back to the beginning of the pool where they started. "What the?" Coach Nelly panicked. "That girl is fast. Let's see what she's got." She then did a flip turn and swam back to the beginning of the pool with Wren. "You can't beat your coach, Wren," she commented, laughing through the water. "You wanna see about that?" Wren also commented and turned her freestyle into a butterfly stroke. "BUTTERFLY!" She screamed, shouting the word like a Magical Girl, ready to attack a villian. "She swapped to the butterfly stroke without taking a break. This girl should be in the Olympics," Coach Nelly amazed.

Wren touched the wall with both of her hands and got out of the pool. "I won," she cheered, giving the swimmers a thumbs up." The crowd went wild, shouting her real name. "WREN! WREN! WREN!"

As for Coach Nelly, she jumped out of the pool and put her hand on Wren's shoulder, turning her around, looking eye to eye. "How did you swap strokes like that without taking a break?" "I do that all of the time at the Athletic Center. I do that to challenge myself after practice," Wren chuckled.

Coach Nelly backed up from Wren and patted her head. "You are something special, Wren. You are the first new swimmer that has moved to the advanced stage without feeling tired and can beat a coach in her own game. I will forever pay my respects to you, Sakura Flowers." She bowed to Wren and raised her arm in the air, facing the swimmers. "WE HAVE AN ADVANCED SWIMMER TO OUR TEAM!" The girls cheered and Wren cried tears of joy. "This is the happiest day of my life," She said to herself, wiping her tears off her face. "See you next week, writer," Coach Nelly said, shaking Wren's hand. "Thank you," she smiled.

5

In the locker room, Wren took off her swimsuit and changed back into her clothes. The three *fangirls* entered the locker room, giving Wren compliments. "Hey guys," Wren greeted. "You were epic out there. You beated the coach," the black-haired girl jumped, giving Wren a tight hug. "You are now the first advanced swimmer on the team," said the brown-haired girl, joining the hug. "Can we be friends, please? You seem like a really cool and nice person to hangout with," said the red-haired girl, sounding a little shy. "Sure," Wren agreed, "The moment I saw all of you reacting to my pen name. I can tell we're going to be good friends." "I don't think we introduced ourselves to you," the red-haired girl said. "I guess I can start," the black-haired girl said, clearing her throat. "My name is Samantha Sail. I'm also 19 years old. I work at Target and I'm in college for Surgical Tech. I like skateboarding and gambling. To be real, I am nervous-nelly." "YOU GAMBLE?!" they all panicked. "Only in card games and sports shows. I'm the youngest gambler in the family." "We can see that," the brown-haired girl laughed, "I'm Bianca Katherine. I'm 18 years old. Working as a dancing instructor and I'm in college for dance. I like to dance and make TikToks. I'm a savage-rebel." "Savage-rebel?" Wren wondered. "If people mess with me, I'll get them back and not give a damn," Bianca responded. "That makes sense," Wren kindly shrugged, giving out a small smirk. "I guess it's my turn," said the red-haired girl, scratching her hair. "My name is Nikki Scott. I'm a 19 year old twitch streamer who loves video games. I'm a peace-maker and secretly a troublemaker." "How are you a troublemaker? You don't look like a troublemaker?" Wren commented. "You'll see it once you know me more." "What kind of bad things did you do in the past?" Samantha excitedly asked. "I changed the water in fire sprinkler systems into blue paint all over my school last year. So I suffered six days in detention for three hours." "WHAT THE HELL?!" they screamed with their eyes and mouths wide open. "We need to keep an eye on you, *Shy-Girl*," Bianca worried, pointing her index finger at her. "I'm carrying my grandma's bible everywhere we go with you," Samantha joked.

"I'm glad we had a chance to introduce ourselves to you," Samantha smiled, holding her hand out, wanting a hand shake. Wren shook her hand. "Me too." "So, now that we're friends. Do we call you Sakura or Wren?" Bianca asked. "You all can call me Wren. Only strangers can call me Sakura." "To know each other more, maybe we can plan our first hangout?" Nikki kindly suggested. "What place should we go?" Bianca wondered. "How about the arcade?" Samantha happily suggested. "Sure, let's go tonight at six," Wren agreed.

They all walked out of the locker room and outside the college and looked at the building. "What do you think of the team, Wren?" Nikki asked. "I'd say I love it here. I feel like I can do anything with all of you," Wren happily responded to Nikki's question. "If you want, you can write a book about us after the Magical Girl Army series," Bianca recommended. "That will be cool. We'll be in an epic series with Sakura Flowers," Samantha thrilled, wrapping her arm around Wren's shoulder. "That's a good idea," Wren agreed. "But what should I call the series?" "Aqua Girl and The Aquatics, Sakura and The Swim Gang, or Swim Warriors, but more cool," Bianca called out the names to her. "I'll think about it, but how am I going to form my experience into a book?" "Try writing in your diary," Nikki quietly said. "Diary?" they all questioned her. "Um…yes…uh…you can write in your diary about your day and fun moments of the team and when you put it all together, you can write it all down into a book. If that's okay with you."

Wren scrolled through her phone and typed the diary and book naming ideas onto her notes app. "Sure, I'll do that, but it won't be done until I'm done with the Magical Girl Army." "DEAL!" They all screamed.

They walked to their own cars, except for Bianca. Bianca sat down, in front of the college door. "Bianca?" Samantha worried. "You don't have a car?" "Nope. I have driving anxiety. So, my mom picks me up from practice until I learn how to drive, but I'll still see you all at the arcade tonight," she waved. "See you later, then," Wren also waved and entered her car. Nikki and Samantha did the same thing and they drove themselves home.

As for Bianca, she scrolled through her contacts on her black iphone 14, looking for her mother's name. She pressed her mom's name and called her. "C'mon, mom. Pick up. My friends are gone and so is everybody else." Her mom picked up the phone. "Hey mom. Are you on your way? Everybody else left and- okay. Where? I don't- oh I see you now." Bianca hung up the phone and her mom picked her up in a gray Jeep.

At home, Wren was telling her family about her first day on the team in the living room. "It was epic, everyone. When I introduced myself, three girls who all became my friends freaked out as soon as they found out I'm Sakura Flowers. Not only that, as a new swimmer, Coach Nelly challenged me to a 50 yd freestyle race. And guess what? I beated her when I turned my freestyle to butterfly at the last minute. She was so impressed, she told me I should be in the Olympics. The crowd went wild and they welcomed me to the team." "That's cool, sweetheart," Mrs.Sky grinned. "I'm glad you like the team. I'm so proud of you," Mr.Sky gave Wren a thumbs up. "Who are your three friends?" Mikayla politely asked. "My friends are Samantha, Bianca, and Nikki," Wren responded. "We talked for a bit after practice. They are really nice. To get to know each other more, we're going to the arcade tonight around six. Do you wanna come?" "Nah, I'll pass," Mikayla shook her hand like a diva. "I don't even know them." "You're lost," Wren shrugged and walked up the stairs, about to take a shower. "I'll be back. I'm about to shower and then take a nap," she told her family.

5:30pm, Wren put on dark brown eyeshadow and mascara. She wore a navy blue hoodie with black ripped-hole jeans. She put the top part of her hair into a low bun and let the back of her hair down with a right bang. "All done," she snapped her fingers at herself in the mirror. "I need one more thing though. Lip gloss and small silver hoop earrings." She put on her hoop earrings and clear, glitter lipgloss. "I'm all set," she smiled.

Mikayla went to the bedroom, grabbing her teal sketchbook and saw Wren fluffing her bun, before heading back downstairs. "Excited for the party, *Eren Yeager?*" She joked, peeking through the bathroom door. "Oh ha-ha," Wren shrugged, putting the brush down on the counter.

Eren Yeager was the main character from *Attack On Titan* from Haijime Isayama. Mikayla called Wren "Eren" because her hairstyle matched Eren's hairstyle from season 4.

The twins walked to the bedroom, and Mikayla watched Wren putting her wallet, phone, inhaler, keys, and bubblegum into her red and brown backpack. "What time will you be home?" "I'll probably be home around nine or ten tonight. I'll text you when I'm on my way home."

They walked downstairs, and Wren put her black and white sneakers on. "I hope you have fun," Mikayla hugged Wren. "Thanks, lil sis." And Wren left the house.

Outside the Arcade, Bianca, Nikki, and Samantha were waiting for Wren. Samantha wore a black glitter dress, down to her knees with black plain leggings underneath and her hair was down. Bianca wore a black shirt with a white skull on it with a black and white plaid skirt and biker shorts underneath. Her hair was in a high poofy ponytail. Nikki wore a teal sweater dress that says _DON'T DISTURB ME! I'M GAMING_ in dark blue ink with dark blue jeans. Her hair was down. The three of them were carrying their own mini purses. Samantha's purse was orange. Bianca's purse was dark purple, and Nikki's purse was teal.

"Anyone see Wren?" Bianca asked, looking at the parking lot. "No," Nikki and Samantha responded, shrugging their shoulders. "Wait, I think I see her," Samantha pointed, seeing Wren parking her silver car in the parking spot. "There's our author," Bianca cheered, hugging Nikki and Samantha tightly.

Wren got out of her car and ran to the entrance of the arcade, where her friends were at. "Guys! Guys! I'm here! I'm here!" she yelled, running towards them. "WREN!" They happily screamed and they gave each other a group hug. "We're gonna have so much fun," Samantha jumped. "What are we waiting for? Let's get in and have some fun," Nikki loudly cheered and they went inside the arcade and played games.

Inside the arcade, the arcade games and the whole building was glowing with neon lights. Including the walls and the floor. Also the doors to the restrooms, laser tag room, and glow golf. The girls' clothes glowed except for Samantha's. She wore a black dress. "Cool, our clothes are glowing," Nikki happily pointed out, looking at her clothes. "Us too," Bianca and Wren said together. "How about you, Sam?" Nikki asked. Samantha looked at her dress. "It's not glowing," she sighed. "Maybe because you're wearing a black dress," Bianca said. "I knew I shouldn't wear black," she pouted. "At least it's a good color on you," Wren complimented, patting Samantha's shoulder. "Let's go play some games," Bianca cheered and they all ran to the games.

For two hours they played: Dance Revolution, Fishy Jackpot, SkeezBall, Pac-Man, Piano-Rush, TrackRacer, Whack-A-Mole, Air Hockey, Spin The Wheel, Plushie crane games, and ball crane games.

They each won one stuffed animal. Wren won a mini pusheen plushie, Samantha won a Eric Cartman plush, Nikki won a Garfield plush and Bianca won a sky blue teddy bear. Only Bianca and Nikki won mini spiky bouncy balls. All four of them earned jackpots. Samantha and Wren won two jackpots. Bianca and Nikki won one jackpot. Other than tickets getting printed out of the games, the tickets were transferred into their cards.

After playing the games, they sat at a table with red chairs, eating a big pepperoni pizza and soda. Samanatha was the only one drinking water. Wren and Bianca were drinking Coke and Nikki was drinking Dr.Pepper.

"What do you think of the hangout, Wren?" Nikki quietly asked. "I'm having a blast. I'm grateful I have great friends like all of you," she replied, getting a second slice of pizza. "Awww," they all said, leaning towards her. "I'm glad we met you too," Samantha nodded, drinking her water. "Can you tell us more about yourself?" Bianca asked. "Sure," she agreed, wiping her greasy hands with a small white napkin. "I have a twin sister. She's the youngest and I'm the oldest. I've been interested in competitive swimming ever since I was a toddler. I joined a team back in high school, but I had to quit because I was put into the wrong age group, plus I wanted to focus on my education, so I practiced more at the Athletic Center until I was transferred to the team." "Do you have a job?" Nikki asked. "Yes, I work as a freelance author at home. It was hard in the beginning because nobody bought my first book, until I wrote my first series which is: The Magical Girl Army. Ever since that series came out, I've been making lots of money on the internet. Plus, people are finally buying my first book I wrote back when I was sixteen." "That's awesome," Samantha cheered, "do you want to become a full-time author one day?" "Yes, I do. I was supposed to be in school for creative writing, until my mom told me I have to do a different career which is dental hygiene because she thought there weren't any schools for creative writing, so as of right now, I'm studying for dental hygiene." "Do you like the dental hygiene program?" Bianca asked.

Wren slightly crushed her cup, and scratched her head out of embarrassment. "I'm…okay with the program, but I don't like the amount of stress it puts on me sometimes. Definitely general studies. At least it'll help me make money on the side. My twin sister is happy I'm studying dental hygiene. She tells me everyday to do writing as a side job, but I want to make it full-time. Overall, I'm kinda okay with the program. As long as it prevents me from being poor." "I hope one day you'll find a school for creative writing," Samantha said, feeling bad. "I will. My family doesn't know, but I've been looking for schools that have my major. Hopefully, they will agree with the idea." "Keep up the hard work," Bianca said, rubbing Wren's head like a dog. "When you find the right school, follow that dream." Wren's eyes watered and she hugged Bianca. "Thank you. I most certainly will."

They all continued eating their pizza until the whole platter was empty without a crumb in sight.

After eating pizza, they threw their plates and cups away in a garbage can by the register. "Damn, that pizza was good," Bianca complimented, rubbing her stomach like she's pregnant. "Before we leave the arcade, you guys wanna trade in our tickets for prizes?" Samantha asked, pointing her right thumb at the prize store. "Sure, let's go," Wren agreed. "I love their prizes." They went inside the prize store and started looking around.

In the prize store, the walls were white with dark blue, green, and purple stripes all over. Bright lights brightened at the kids, teenagers, and employees, and each shelf had stuffed animals, big and small candy, light up teeth and pacifiers, workout accessories, t-shirts and sweaters, mini cups and big water bottles, and slappable bracelets.

Wren was in the toy aisle, Samantha was in the candy aisle, Bianca was in the water bottle aisle, and Nikki was in the t-shirt and sweater aisle.

Wren wondered what to buy. "So many options," she muttered. "Do I have enough tickets?" She then looked at a mini Sonic figure in a box, next to a giant Sonic plush. "No way, they have the figure. I've always wanted a Sonic figure. I can use it as a pocket pet." She grabbed the sonic figure and ran to the other aisles with her friends.

Few minutes later, the girls walked out of the prize store, showing each other what they bought. Samantha bought a blueberry WarHeads spray with a LED mouthguard. Nikki bought a dark and light blue striped-knitted sweater, gray neck pillow, and a clear water bottle with a gaming console on it. Bianca only bought a mini console with 350+ games inside it. Wren bought a mini Sonic figure, three packs of bubble gum cigarettes, and pink and blue LED pacifiers. "We should come here more often," Wren commented. "No kidding," Nikki agreed.

They walked out of the arcade, giving each other a goodbye group hug. "I'm glad we met. I had a wonderful time with all of you," Wren smiled. "Me too. I'm glad we met an amazing author and swimmer into our group," Bianca said. Nikki walked close to Wren, holding her hands. "Can we hangout more often, please?" she quietly said. Samantha and Bianca walked behind her, cupping their hands up to their ears. "What did you say?" They both questioned. "Can we hangout more often, please?" She raised her voice. Bianca and Samantha finally understood her. "Yes, we can. You all earn my friendship," Wren smiled, rubbing Nikki's head.

Bianca heard her phone vibrate in her purse and looked to see who was texting her. "My mom's coming to the parking lot, guys," She said, "see you all at practice." "Bye, Bianca. Bye guys," Wren waved, walking backwards to her car. "Bye Wren," they waved back and walked to their cars.

Wren got in her car and looked at her bag full of prizes she won from the arcade. "This is a blessing," she smiled. She dug inside of her prize bag and pulled out a white box of bubble gum cigarettes. She opened the box and put a cherry bubblegum cigarette in her mouth. "This is more like it." And drove herself home.

6

In Coach Nelly's office at the Athletic Community College, Coach Nelly was on her computer, typing a calendar of events for the girls to keep. She printed the papers out of her black printer and stacked them together, next to her white coffee mug that says **Best Coach Ever**. "All done," she sighed, taking a little sip of her coffee. "This month's and next month's calendars. I just need to give them to the girls and prepare them for our first swim meet."

She put her coffee mug down on her desk and saw a USPS worker, knocking through her large glass window. "A package? I don't remember ordering a package. Or did I?" She walked out of her office and the USPS worker gave her a giant box. "Package for you?" he said, sounding tired and angry. "Thank you," Coach Nelly smiled and the USPS worker walked out of the building.

Coach Nelly walked back to her desk and put the box on her navy blue chair. She grabbed her big red scissors and cut the box open.

Inside the box, there were different sized sky blue jackets written **SWORDFISH TEAM** in navy blue ink with a picture of an angry swordfish balled up in the middle of the logo. Coach Nelly took the large-sized jacket out of the box, sat it on top of her black keyboard, and took a picture of it with her purple iphone. "I can't wait to give these to the girls," she smiled, sending the picture to the team email for the girls to see.

After taking the picture, she put the jacket back in the box and put the box in front of her desk.

At home, Wren was at the kitchen table, doing her homework assignments. "This is too much," she complained. "This dental program better be worth it. With the money I'll make as a dental hygienist, I will use it to save up to move out and become a full-time writer. But how do I become a full-time writer, though?"

Wren gently tapped her blue mechanical pencil on her notebook multiple times until she saw her phone vibrating next to her pink laptop. She picked up her phone and saw Coach Nelly's name on her Gmail notifications. *An email from the coach. Practice isn't until tomorrow.* She opened the email and saw a picture of the team jacket Coach Nelly ordered. "Oh my sweet Jesus!" Wren gasped, covering her mouth with her hand. "We're getting Jackets!" she squealed, slamming her blue mechanical pencil onto her notebook. "I gotta show mom, dad, and Mikayla this, but first I need to continue with my homework." She put her phone down on the table and continued doing her homework.

7

At swim practice, the girls were lined up in a straight line, wearing their swimsuits, while Coach Nelly was getting the box of team jackets out of her office. Wren and Nikki wore their own colored camouflage swimsuits. Wren's swimsuit was pink and Nikki's was teal. Bianca wore a plain violet swimsuit. Samantha wore a yellow and black striped swimsuit. Bianca gave out a small laugh. Samantha felt embarrassed. "What?" Samantha questioned, seeing Bianca's face turning red. "Are you a bumblebee?" "A what?" "Your swimsuit. You look like a bumblebee," she laughed. "As you can see, yellow and black are my favorite colors. So I'm wearing a swimsuit that has my favorite colors."

Nikki and Wren looked over at Bianca and Samantha and joined their conversation. "If you're wearing a black and yellow swimsuit, can you do the bumblebee dance?" Wren happily suggested. "HELL NO!" yelled Samantha, crossing her arms and turning away from her friends.

"Please, for us? Coach Nelly is still in her office," Nikki begged. Samantha turned her back around to her friends and gave out a frustrating sigh. "Show me the money," she said.

Bianca walked to her light purple swim bag and gave Samantha a fifty dollar bill. "Is this enough?" asked Bianca. Samantha took the fifty dollar bill and put it in her bag. "Let's get this over with."

Samantha stood in front of everybody and sang and danced to the BumbleBee song. "Sweet little bumblebee. I know what you want from me. Doo-bi-doo-bi, doo-da-da. Doo-bi-doo-bi, doo-da-da."

Wren, Nikki, Bianca, and the rest of the team laughed at Samantha. Bianca recorded her on her phone. Samantha stopped dancing and screamed. "SCREW ALL OF YOU! I HATE YOU GUYS!" Wren, Bianca, and Nikki hugged Samantha after laughing. "We're sorry, Sam," they apologized. "I forgive you guys. It was funny anyway," she muttered, hugging them back.

Coach Nelly walked out of her office with the box of team jackets. "What's in the box, coach?" Samantha asked. Coach Nelly slammed the box down in front of the girls and looked at Samantha, trying not to laugh. "Why do you look like a bumblebee?" she asked. "Shut up," Samantha shushed her.

Coach Nelly blew her whistle at the girls, grabbing their attention. "Great news, ladies. We finally got our team jackets." The girls screamed out of excitement. They screamed so loud, Coach Nelly quickly covered her ears. "I thought my whistle was the loudest in this building," she commented, shrugging her shoulders. "But…you all won't get your jackets until the end of the day." "Awww!" They all complained, hoping they were getting their jackets before practice. "I do have a big announcement," Coach Nelly continued. "We have our first medley race a week after next week. It's going to be at a Dearborn Athletic Center. We're competing up against the Sharks." "THE SHARKS?!" They Jumped. "I can tell all of you think the team name sounds silly, I know. But they are actually hardcore and mean." "Uh oh," Nikki gulped. "'Uh-oh,' indeed. That is why for today and next week we're gonna practice until we feel confident to beat them," Coach Nelly said. "Today, you're going to split into a group of four to practice your strokes to see which one of you is better at doing the stroke for our first swim meet."

The swimmers looked at each other, eye to eye. Knowing who will be in their groups.

Coach Nelly walked in front of Wren, patting her head. "How do you feel about *your* first swim meet, kiddo?" Wren couldn't answer Coach Nelly's question. Her heart was racing five times faster, ready to have a heart attack. She was sweating like she was in a volcano, and feeling like she can't breathe. Coach Nelly snapped her fingers to Wren's ears, snapping her out of it. "Sakura? Are you okay?" Wren shook her head, waking herself up. "Yes, I'm okay," she replied, rubbing her head. "Just nervous about my first swim meet."

Coach Nelly wrapped her arm around Wren and gave her a calming quote about the swim meet. "No pressure, girl. Don't think you have to be perfect. Don't ever think you're not worthy enough to battle. It may sound scary, but as soon as you walk on the battlefield, you'll feel like you can fight like a brave warrior. You know what I'm saying?" Wren confidently nodded her head and gave out a proud smile. "You're right. I'll be fine. Besides, it's not the end of the world if we lose, there's always next time battles. Thank you, coach." "Your welcome, Wren."

Bianca, Samantha, and Nikki worriedly looked at Wren. "Are you okay?" Nikki quietly asked. "Yes, I'm okay. Just a little panic attack. It's normal. I just have anxiety. Don't worry about me, I'm fine." "Okay, just as long you're fine," said Samantha, giving Wren a thumbs up. "While you were talking to Coach Nelly, we decided for all of us to be in a group of four," Bianca said, excitedly shaking Wren. "If that's okay with you. Right Bianca?" said Nikki, purposely correcting Bianca. "Right. If it's okay with you," She sweated. "Sure. I don't mind. I was thinking the same thing when the coach talked about splitting us into groups of four," Wren agreed. "I have one question," Samantha raised her hand to Wren like a student, "are we picking our swimming positions or Coach Nelly will?" "Coach Nelly will be the one picking our positions," Wren repiled. "DAMN IT!" Samantha, Nikki, and Bianca yelled, slamming their bare feet to the ground.

Coach Nelly blew her whistle again and the swimmers turned their heads towards her. "Did you all pick your groups?" "YES!" They all said. "Good Job, everybody. Now, I want all of you to practice freestyle, backstroke, breaststroke, and butterfly for twenty minutes so I can pick your positions for our relay and Medley race."

The swimmers and their groups got into their own lanes and started practicing the positions.

As for Coach Nelly, she grabbed the whiteboard and started labeling positions for the girls.

Two hours later, Coach Nelly blew her whistle to get the girls out of the pool. "Time's up, ladies. Get out of the pool and get ready to hear your positions." The swimmers got out of the pool and sat on the floor, looking at Coach

Nelly and the whiteboard with their names and positions written in blue marker.

"After seeing you girls swim with the four strokes. I've already picked out your positions. When I call your name and the position you're doing. You have to do it for the sake of our team. Samantha, Tanya, and Katherine, you three are assigned to do freestyle. Bianca, Kayla, and Ruby, you three are assigned to do backstroke. Nikki, Susie, and Keisha, you three are assigned to do breaststroke. Wren, Tammy, and Sonia, you three are assigned to do butterfly. You cannot switch positions with each other. I hope you all practice outside the building and we'll practice more of your strokes next week. Have a nice day."

The swimmers got up from the ground and changed into their clothes in the locker room.

After they changed into their clothes, Wren, Samantha, Nikki, and Bianca walked out of the ACC together, talking about their relay race group and their positions. "To be honest, I'm not surprised that Coach

Nelly gave me a hard stroke to do," said Wren, getting her car keys out of her swim bag. "I'm so glad she gave me the easiest stroke. I can win easily doing freestyle," Samantha happily cheered. "I'm okay with any stroke," Nikki shrugged. "As long as she doesn't give me butterfly and breaststroke, I will most definitely win," Bianca commented. "Now that we're in a group, you think we should have our own group name?" Wren suggested. "We can't be a group without a name." "Wren's right. We need to name this group," Nikki quietly agreed with Wren. "How about we can call ourselves *The Swim Warriors*?" Bianca suggested. "I love that name alot," Wren nodded her head. "Same," Nikki quietly said. "Swim Warriors it is," Samantha jumped. "See you all next week," she waved. "BYE!" They all waved and walked back to their cars. Except for Bianca, she's waiting for her mom to pick her up. "I really need to start practicing driving now," she complained, looking at her pink watch on her right wrist.

8

Wren came home from practice, feeling tired and exhausted. Mr.Sky, Mrs.Sky, and Mikayla asked her about her day at practice. Wren told them practice was good and they have a swim meet a week after next week. She told them the description and location of the swim meet and they were excited. Mikayla felt a little excited, but nervous at the same time.

After she told her family about her first swim meet, Wren took a shower and went to her room to take a nap.

Throughout the whole week, Wren had been doing competitive workouts to boost her energy and strength in the theater room in the basement. She ran up and down the stairs, lifted ten through twenty pounds of dumbbells, jump-rope, sit-ups, push-ups, boxing her punchbag, and jogging in place.

After her intensive workout, she did yoga for twenty minutes to avoid her anxiety getting in the way. After that, she rolled up her yoga mat and put it in the corner by the theater room tv. "Wow!" She was amazed. "What a workout. This calls for a shower," she snapped her fingers.

She walked upstairs to her bathroom and took a steamy, hot shower. After the shower, she sat on top of a toilet, air drying.

After getting dressed, Wren walked downstairs, in the living room, and watched tv with Mikayla.

Fifthteen minutes later, Wren got a text from Samantha.

Samantha: Hey Wren. Do you still practice at the Athletic Center?

Wren raised an eyebrow and texted Samantha back.

Wren: Sometimes. Why?

Samantha: I was wondering if we all can practice over there.

Wren: Sure, we can still practice, but we have to pay $15 for each person.

Samantha: Deal. What time do you want to go?

Wren: We can go now, but we need to tell Nikki and Bianca.

Samantha: OK. I'll tell them.

Wren: Thank you.

Wren stood up from the couch and went to the closet and grabbed her jacket and car keys.

Mikayla gazed at Wren and asked her where she was going. "Where are you going, Wren?" "I just got a text from Sam. We're going to practice our strokes at the Athletic Center." Mikayla gave out a sad sounding sigh and face palmed. "Come on, Wren," she complained. "It's not that serious. Over a competition?" "Mikayla, we need to practice in order to beat 'The Sharks.'"

When Wren told Mikayla the name of the team they were up against, Mikayla looked at Wren like she was crazy as if she made up the name. "Are you high or something, sis?" She was worried. "No, I am not high," Wren chuckled. "That's actually the name of the team we're competing with."

"Did their coach smoke something when she was making her own team?"

"I honestly do not know."

"Are there actually teams with corny-ass names?"

"Yes, but there are some that actually live up to their team names."

"Alright," Mikayla laughed. "Anyway, have fun."

"Thanks, Mikayla. I'll be home in an hour or two." Wren left the house and drove to the Athletic Center.

At the Athletic Center, Wren saw Sam and Nikki standing in front of the entrance door. She got out of her car and walked towards them. "Hey guys, where's Bianca?" she asked. "Bianca said she'll be running late because her mom is coming home from work," Nikki quietly responded, brushing her red hair with her hands. "Should we just go in and let her know we're in the pool area because it's starting to get cold and I don't want any of us to get sick before the competition," Samantha politely suggested. "Sure, let's do that," Wren agreed. They walked inside the building, paid for their pool visits, and changed into their swimsuits in the locker room. Before Nikki changed into her swimsuit. She texted Bianca that her, Samantha, and Wren were already changing into their swimsuits and to meet them in the pool area.

After changing into their swimsuits, the three of them walked out of the locker room and entered the pool area.

The three of them were wearing their same training swimsuits from last practice. Nikki and Wren continued to laugh at Samantha's *bumblebee* swimsuit. "SCREW YOU GUYS!" She screamed, raised a fist in their faces.

After their little laughter, they splitted into their own lanes and swam with the strokes Coach Nelly assigned them.

Meanwhile with Bianca, she was sitting outside on her porch with her swim bag next to her, waiting for her mom. "Where the hell are you, mom?" she complained.

HONK! HONK! Bianca's mom arrived. "Finally," she cheered, and walked to her mom's car. "Sorry I'm late sweety. I had to get coffee with my friends."

Bianca's mom wore a black skinny suit over her white long-sleeve button shirt. Her Hair was in a bun and had freckles all over her face.

While Bianca's mom drove her to the Athletic Center, she talked to Bianca about getting a license. "Sweetheart, when are you going to practice how to drive?" Bianca shrugged her shoulders and said, "I don't know. I'm too scared to drive." Bianca's mom patted Bianca's head and gave out a stressful sigh. "Honey, I know driving can be scary, but driving can take you anywhere where you'll feel independent and adventurous." Bianca looked at her mom as if she had lobsters crawling out of her ears. "What are you saying?" Bianca questioned her with a mean attitude. Her mother didn't like the attitude Bianca gave her. "What I'm saying is you need to learn someday so you drive yourself to your team events and learn not to talk to me like that or else I'll kick you off the team." "Yes, ma'am. Sorry," she gulped. "When do you want to start practicing?" "Maybe when the swimming season is over. Especially that I need to focus more on my college education."

Bianca's mom parked in front of the Athletic Center and Bianca ran into the building, paid for her pool visit, and quickly changed into her swimsuit. She also wore the same swimsuit from last practice, went to the pool area, and saw her friends swimming in their own lanes. "I'm here, girls," she screamed.

Samantha, Wren, and Nikki heard Bianca's voice while they were in the pool. They stopped swimming and waved their arms at her. "Hey Bianca. Come join us," they happily cheered. Bianca jumped into the last lane by the wall and started practicing her stroke.

Samantha was practicing freestyle, Wren was practicing butterfly, Nikki was practicing breaststroke, and Bianca was practicing Backstroke. The four of them practiced their strokes for two hours, until they felt tired and proud.

After practicing their strokes, Wren got out of the pool and gave her friends blue kickboards and they practiced their kicks.

The kicks they practiced were the dolphin kicks, mermaid kicks, and the breaststroke kicks. After practicing their kicks. They got out of the pool and took a 'water break.'

During their 'water break,' a yellow light bulb popped above Samantha's head and she loudly slammed her tall blue water bottle onto the bench, scaring Wren, Bianca, and Nikki. The three of them turned their heads towards her. "Everything alright?" Nikki quietly asked. "Yes, I'm fine," she cheered. "How about we can have a race?" "A race?" Wren questioned, "what kind of race?" "Let's have an individual race with the strokes Coach Nelly assigned us. A 50 yd race."

Wren, Bianca, and Nikki looked at each other then looked at the clock that was across the room. "Sure, let's have a race?" Wren agreed. "Agree," Nikki and Bianca also agreed. "Great, but there is a stake?" "A stake?" Bianca nervously asked. "I think I'm gonna piss myself," Nikki gulped, shaking in fear. "Whoever loses the individual race, will have to do the bumblebee dance." Wren, Bianca, and Nikki gave out a little chuckle. They were thinking about Samantha doing the bumblebee dance from their previous swim practice. Samantha knew why they were chuckling. "Fine. Go ahead and laugh," she sighed. And the three of them started to laugh. They laughed so hard, they fell on the ground, balled up, holding their stomachs. "Was it really that funny?" Samantha's face turned red. "HELL YEAH IT WAS!" They shouted and continued laughing.

Samantha walked across the pool where a black-haired boy employee with a name tag that read *Timothy* was at and snatched the whistle from around his neck, telling him "I'm going to need this, sir. My friends are total idiots today." She walked back to the other side of the pool and blew the whistle into their ears. "AHHHHHHH! MY EARS!" they panicked, covering their ears. "Are you guys done?" she politely asked, swang the whistle around. Wren, Bianca, and Nikki stood up from the ground, bowed to Samantha out of respect. "Sorry, Sam," they apologized.

Timothy the lifeguard walked towards Samantha, snatching the whistle out of her hand. "Do that again and you'll be banned." And walked back to the other side of the pool. "Did you just take Timothy's whistle?" Wren asked, pointing her finger at him. "Yeah, why?" "Lifeguards and coaches don't like that. If you do that to them it will piss them off. If you do it more often, you will be kicked out for months." Samantha gazed at Wren like she made up the rules. "Is there some kind of policy?" "Yes, there is." Wren pointed to the policy that was taped on the glass door to the locker rooms. "Huh? Well I'll be damned," Samantha shook her head. "Well, let's race shall we."

The Swim Warriors jumped back into their same pool lanes and formed into their starting positions. Except for Bianca. She faced towards the wall so she could swim on her back. Everyone else was faced towards the other side of the pool. Samantha started the countdown. "On your mark…get set…GO!" They swam underwater with a dolphin kick, swarmed above the water, and started swimming with their strokes.

Wren was already in the lead. Nikki was behind her and Bianca was behind Nikki. Samantha was coming into last place. *NO! NO! NO! I can't let them beat me.* Wren, Bianca, and Nikki touched the wall and flip-turned back to the beginning of the lane. Samantha saw them swimming back. She started to sob in her head. *It's not fair, I can't let them beat me. AHHHH!* She did a flip-turn and followed her friends.

Back to the beginning of the wall, Wren beated her friends in first place. Bianca was placed in second place. Nikki was placed in third place. Sadly, Samantha was placed in fourth place. Samantha knew she was screwed. She couldn't see her friends' legs in the pool. She touched the wall and got out of the pool feeling embarrassed. "I'm guessing I have to do the bumblebee dance?" she assumed. Wren, Bianca, and Nikki looked at each other with big grins on their faces and raised their hands up for a high five. "Good job, Sam. Nice race," Wren smiled. "Oh Wow! No dance?" she wondered, giving her friends high fives. "You will still dance," Bianca said, "But why not dance together as a victory dance." "You mean that?" Samantha smiled. "Sure, we're warriors. We need to celebrate this moment." "How about we do the victory dance at our first swim meet?" Nikki quietly suggested. "I'd say that's a good idea," Wren agreed.

Bianca was okay with the idea, but at the same time she wasn't. She still wants to celebrate their hard work. "If no one wants to do a victory dance, how are we going to celebrate our hard work?" She asked. Samantha, Nikki, and Wren started to think, until they yelled, "STARBUCKS!" Bianca nodded her head. "That's not a bad idea, but I don't have a ride." "It's okay," Wren said, wrapping her arm around her shoulders, "you can drive with me." "I can drive you home since we live close," Nikki also joined, wrapping both of her arms around Bianca. "Thanks, guys. You're the best," Bianca smiled, hugging Wren and Nikki.

After Bianca's mother talked to her about getting a license, Bianca was not in the mood to call her mom to take her to Starbucks with her friends. It's not the first time her mom talked to her about getting a license. This has been going on since she started college. Whenever she was not in the mood to drive with her mom, driving with her friends was the only way out.

"Let's change clothes first and then go to Starbucks," Samantha suggested. They changed into their casual clothes and went outside to their cars. Bianca's driving with Wren and they all drove to Starbucks to celebrate their hard work.

9

Saturday evening, Wren was getting dressed in the bathroom for her first swim meet. She wore her pink and red camouflage swimsuit underneath her navy blue jumpsuit. She put her in a high bun with a left bang and drew three blue stars on her right cheek like she was a rockstar.

After getting dressed, she looked in the mirror, took a deep breath and reminded herself to calm down. "Calm down, Wren. No pressure. Don't think negatively. Just do what you have to do. Believe in yourself and have fun." She walked out of the bathroom, grabbed her swim bag, and ran downstairs where Mikayla, and her parents were at.

In the living room, Mikayla, Mr. and Mrs.Sky wore a sky blue shirt written in white ink that read *Swim Warriors* with a shield and a sword on the back of it. Wren was so amazed by the shirts, she'd nearly cried tears of joy.

"W-w-w-w-w-" Wren was speechless. She can't stop staring at their shirts. "Do you like them, sweetheart? It represents your group," Mrs.Sky said, showing Wren her shirt. Wren continued to stutter. "W-w-w-w-" "Sounds like she's speechless,"Mr.Sky whispered in Mrs.Sky's ear. "What? How? When? How did you guys know the name of my group?" Mr.Sky and Mrs.Sky slowly looked at Mikayla. Mikayla looked back at them a little mad. "Why are you guys looking at me?" "You know why," Mr.Sky said, nudging her shoulder with his hand. Mikayla still felt confused until she figured it out. "Oh! That's right. Remember how you told me you and your friends call yourselves *The Swim Warriors*?" "I don't think I told you," Wren shook her head. "I told mom and dad and they decided to make shirts to support you." "Aww, Thanks," Wren smiled and gave her family a hug. "But seriously, how did you know my group name?" Wren politely repeated her question. "Well…" Mikayla rolled her eyes, tapping her fingers together, "I read your text messages when you were in the shower last week." "YOU DID

WHAT?!" Wren freaked out. "If you want the name of my group, just ask." "Okay, then," Mikayla shrugged, sounding like it wasn't a big deal even though it was.

Mr.Sky looked at his watch and asked Wren what time is her swim meet. "What time is the swim meet?" Wren looked at her phone and replied, "It starts at 4:30pm. It's 4:00 pm." "Do you think we should leave now?" Mrs.Sky asked. "Yeah, let's do that so she can change and be prepared for her first battle," Mr.Sky agreed, pulling his keys out of his pocket. They put on their jackets, walked out of the house and entered Mrs.Sky's gray-ish silver van. Mikayla and Wren wore their fuzzy gray jackets. Mr and Mrs.Sky wore their black fuzzy jackets.

On their way to the swim meet, Wren felt butterflies in her stomach, ready to throw up. Not only did she have to swim to win, there'll be a thousand eyes looking at her and her team. To calm her nerves, she played her favorite song *Hall Of Fame by The Script.* She played the song over and over until they made it to their destination.

Mr.Sky parked the car close to the entrance of the Dearborn Athletic Center and they walked inside the building.

Inside the building, there was a huge amount of people sitting on the bleachers, surrounding the pool. The pool was sparkling and clear and the whole pool stadium was blue and gray. "Is this the right place?" Mikayla asked Wren, "it looks like we're in the olympics." "Yes, this is the right place," said a familiar voice, in an excited tone. "Who was that?" Mikayla jumped. Wren and her family looked at Coach Nelly who was sitting on a bench, in front of the bleachers. Wren and her family walked close to her, asking her some questions. "Who are you?" Mikayla politely asked. "I'm Coach Nelly. I'm your daughter's coach. And you're in the right place. Wren, did you tell your family how you beated me on your first day?" "Yes, I told them. They were shocked," Wren laughed. "Your daughter swims like an olympian. She should join the Olympics someday. It was her first day showing up for practice and she's already in the advanced stage. She's going to be a pro," Coach Nelly bragged, causing Wren to smile and blush. Mikayla gave Wren the side eye and smirked. "You can't handle too many compliments, sis?" "This is too much. I'm going to die from happiness." "Anyway," Coach Nelly continued, clapping her hands together. "Wren, you can change in the changing room and you all can sit on the bleachers with the rest of the crowd." "Thank you," Wren smiled. Wren ran to the womens' changing room and Mikayla and her parents sat in the front of the bleachers. "Do you guys think Wren will win?" Mikayla asked. "She will," Mr.Sky said, giving her a thumbs up, "Let's stay positive for her."

In the womens' changing room, Wren was changing into her pink and red camouflage swimsuit with her friends, teammates, and other swimmers from the other teams. Including the Sharks team. Their worst enemy.

While Wren was changing into her swimsuit, Samantha, Bianca, and Nikki walked towards her with big smiles on their faces. "Are you ready for your first battle, Wren?" Bianca excitedly asked, hugging Wren tightly.

"Yes, I'm excited. I'm happy to see my parents and my twin sister watching me compete at a giant stadium." "Wait, you have a twin sister?" Samantha shook. "Yes, I do. Remember I told you guys when we first met," Wren laughed. "Can we see her, please," Nikki quietly asked. "Sure, I'll show you guys."

Samantha, Bianca, and Nikki followed Wren to the door of the changing room. They poked their heads out of the door and saw Mikayla on her phone, waiting for the swim meet to begin. Samantha, Bianca, and Nikki paused and looked back at Wren and Mikayla a hundred times. "What?" Wren shrugged. "THAT'S YOUR TWIN SISTER?!" "Yeah," she laughed. "YOU GUY DON'T EVEN LOOK LIKE TWINS?! IS SHE YOUR COUSIN OR STEP-SISTER?!" "OF COURSE WE'RE TWINS! WE'RE VETERNIAL TWINS!" Wren shouted back and they all went back inside the changing room. "There is no way that's your twin sister," Bianca said, massaging her forehead like she hit her head. "Yes we are twins. I'm the oldest by two minutes and she's the youngest. A lot of people don't believe that we're twins.

People always assume that we're cousins or friends," Wren explained, digging inside her swim bag, grabbing her swim goggles and swim cap. "Ouch! Doesn't that hurt your feelings?" Nikki wondered. "Not really. It is funny to me. The thing I do hate is twin stereotypes. Everytime people find out that we're twins, they go with the stereotypes of matching clothes, evil or good twins, what twins should look like, and the same personalities. People just don't know that twins can have their own lives without each other sometimes." "I honestly don't blame you," Samantha agreed. "Me too. If I ever have a twin and we have to deal with people like that, I will lose my mind and hurt them," Bianca also agreed, patting Wren's head like she's a dog again. "Sorry if we offended you," Nikki apologized, feeling guilty. "Don't worry, you guys didn't offended me. I'm happy you guys saw my sister and I'm laughing the way you guys looked at us. So to end this conversation, that's Mikayla. She's my twin sister. And I love her." And they all laughed.

During their laughter, a blonde-haired girl with blue eyes and really short hair in the back with a right side bang, wearing a green camouflage swimsuit, mocked their laughs in a sassy tone. "You all laugh like a bunch of nerds." "Oh it's *her* again," Bianca rolled her eyes. "Who is she?" Wren kindly asked. "Her name is-" "The name's Emily. Emily Bandit," Emily rudely interrupted Bianca, "I'm from the Sharks team. And I'm doing the butterfly stroke with my crew. Who's the new girl? And why is she competing today? Isn't she supposed to be in the beginning stage?"

The *new girl* Emily was talking about was Wren. Samantha, Bianca, and Nikki were confused at first, until they found out she was talking about Wren. "Her name is Wren Sky," Samantha kindly introduced Wren to Emily. "She's a college student studying for dental hygiene and an author who goes by a pen name, Sakura Flowers," Bianca also introduced. "She may be a newbie, but she has moved to an advanced stage," Nikki joined the introduction.

Emily smacked her lips and slowly walked around Wren, looking at her body shape and face. "This girl is in an advanced stage. Her face doesn't match her body." "What the hell do you mean?" Bianca fussed, ready to fight her. "She has an innocent and pretty face, but her body seems a little muscular. She has to be a square or something."

The word *square* triggered Wren so badly, she grabbed Emily by her hair and put her close to her face. "Why don't you say that to my face YOU DUMBASS BITCH!" And roughly letting go of Emily, pushing her to the blue lockers. Samantha, Bianca, and Nikki shook in fear, looking at Wren and Emily. "Now that's a real tomboy right there," Samantha commented. "That's our friend til the end," Bianca laughed. "Emily should've stayed away from her," Nikki shook her head in disappointment.

Emily scratched the back of her head and straightened her back. "Damn, you're strong. Where did you get that mighty from?" She panicked. "I got my anger and strength from my father, but I have my golden heart from my mother. I will be nice to you, but if you bully me for no reason, we're going to have a problem," Wren angrily responded.

Emily walked close to Wren's face again with her arms crossed and a smirk on her face. "I have a *simple* question. What's your stroke for this meet?" "I'm doing butterfly," Wren politely replied. "Huh? No shit. I see why. Well, just so you know, you'll be competing against me. Let's see who is the strongest swimmer in this competition." "Bring it on, bitch," Wren also smirked. Emily walked away from Wren and left the womens' changing room with the rest of her team, the other teams, and a few members from the Swordfish team.

Samantha, Bianca, and Nikki worriedly looked at Wren, wondering if she was okay. "Are you okay, Wren?" Samantha panicked, putting both of her hands on Wren's shoulders. "Yeah, I'm okay. Why?" she asked as if the argument never happened. "Emily offended you and your temper got out of control," Nikki nervously asked, tapping both of her index fingers together. "I'm okay. I just had to stand up for myself. Do you all know her? When she mocked us, you guys reacted like you knew her. Were you guys friends or something?" Samantha, Bianca, and Nikki looked nervous telling Wren about Emily until they sighed and made Wren sit on the bench by the lockers.

"Emily was never our friend nor on our team. She's always been like this ever since we met at swim camp. Whenever she sees people who have moved up to the advanced stage, she wants to beat them just to take their title even though it's pointless. She's still in the beginning stage because she's still learning how to do the techniques," Samantha explained, sounding a little sad. "What happened during swim camp?" Wren wondered. Nikki sat behind Wren and told her the story. "Back then, it was only me, Samantha, and Bianca. During swim camp, Coach Nelly wanted us to have a medley race. One of the girls named, Sarah Thompson, was picked to do the butterfly stroke like you, Wren. Emily was also picked to do the butterfly stroke while she was on a different team.

Sarah was advanced. When it was their turn to race, Sarah beated Emily. Emily didn't take the 'L' so well. She'd rematched Sarah, but Sarah won again. Emily was so angry, she…she…she…" Nikki started to panic. "Breathe, Nikki. Breathe. I understand it's traumatizing. You don't have to say it," Bianca comforted her. Nikki took some deep breaths and continued the story. "She broke Sarah's arm and pushed her into the water. Emily was kicked out of camp for the whole summer and Sarah never came back to swimming since." Wren loudly gasped and started shaking in fear. "Where's Sarah now?" she asked. "I checked her Instagram and she's on a soccer team after her arm got better. I remembered her telling us that she was also interested in soccer but she wanted to do more swimming. I'm glad she's doing well now," Bianca happily replied.

Wren felt bad and scared after hearing what happened to Sarah Thompson, but at the same time, she realized that won't stop her from competing against Emily. She knew competing with Emily is going to be a

50/50 percent chance of either winning and getting into a rematch or losing and taking the "L."

"Well…now I know what Emily is capable of doing to me if I win, I'll be ready for whatever happens to me," said Wren, sounding confident. Samantha, Bianca, and Nikki gulped and gave her a thumbs up with fake smiles on their faces. "If she ever tries to hurt you, we'll be ready to kick her ass," Bianca said, cracking her knuckles. "You're right," Samantha agreed, "We won't make the same mistake like at swim camp. We don't want to lose another best friend." "Thank you all," Wren smiled.

Coach Nelly ran inside the womens' changing room, screaming at Wren and her friends. "WHAT ARE YOU GIRLS DOING?! THE MEET IS ABOUT TO START!" "OH CRAP! SORRY!" They apologized and they ran out of the changing room with Coach Nelly.

Wren, Samantha, Bianca, and Nikki lined up with their team and a man wearing a dark blue polo shirt with navy blue pants, started announcing the swim meet.

"Ladies and Gentlemen, welcome to our first swim meet in 2023! Introducing The Swordfish vs The Sharks." Everybody gave both of the teams a round of applause. The right side of the bleachers had people cheering for The Sharks. The left side of the bleachers had people including Wren's, Samantha's, Bianca's, and Nikki's parents, cheering them on with a sky blue poster that read *GO SWIM WARRIORS!* In black marker. Wren, Samantha, Bianca, and Nikki turned around and looked at their parents holding a sign with their group name on it. They waved at their families, smiling and thanking them for making the beautiful sign. "Looks like we have some fans in our hands," Wren commented. "This is the best part about coming to a swim meet," said Samantha, turning her body around, facing towards The Sharks team. Wren, Bianca, and Nikki also turned their bodies too.

"Today's first race will be a medley race," the announcer continued. "Before we get started with the race, we're going to let our swimmers warm up for twenty minutes. Please be patient and we will start our battle shortly."

Coach Nelly and the Sharks Team coach named, Coach Mandy blew their whistles at their own teams and made the girls do push-ups, sit-ups, squats, and punches.

After their warm-ups, Coach Nelly gave the girls a motivational speech. "Listen, Ladies. This is our first swim meet together. Especially with a newbie, Wren. Don't think too much about this whole swim meet. Think about winning, who are you doing this for, and have fun. If you lose this meet, don't feel bad. There's always next time and don't let The Sharks bully you for losing. Everyone makes mistakes. We'll be fine. Alright?" "YES MA'AM!" They screamed.

Coach Mandy also gave The Sharks a *somewhat* motivational speech. "Alright, Sharks. You see them wimps over there. I want you to kick their ass and show who's boss. Don't fail me or else you'll be called a 'baby shark.'" The Sharks cracked their knuckles and smirked at The Swordfish team. "Don't worry, Coach Mandy. We'll kick their ass. We'll kick their ass really good," Emily laughed, staring at Wren with red eyes.

The Swordfish and Sharks team split into groups and rounds. Round One was a 4 x 50 yd race. Wren's group and Emily's group were first to compete. The first people to compete first were the backstroke people. In the Swim Warriors group, Bianca was chosen to be first. She stood on the starting block with the Sharks and the rest of the swimmers and her friends were standing behind her, waiting for their turn to swim. Without thinking, The announcer started the race by honking a loud horn through the speakers, causing the audience and swimmers to cover their ears. "Sorry folks," he apologized and the backstroke swimmers dove into the pool.

Bianca swam ahead from the other swimmers, did a flip turn, and swam back to the starting lane. Wren, Samantha, and Nikki cheered her on as they saw her beating the rest of the backstroke swimmers. Bianca touched the wall, grabbed onto the handle of the block, and Samantha dove into the pool, doing freestyle. "GOD

DAMN IT!" Emily yelled, staring at Wren's group. "YOU IDIOTS WON'T WIN THIS ROUND!" Wren looked at her, teasing her with a big smile on her face.

The rest of the backstroke swimmers got out of the pool and the freestyle swimmers jumped in, but they were swimming behind Samantha. Samantha was swimming so fast, she flipped back to the starting lane, beating the other freestyle swimmers.

Emily looked at Samantha swimming back to the wall towards Nikki and looked at Wren again. "I swear to god if you guys win this round, I'm going to drown you," she threatened, causing Wren to roll her eyes like it was nothing.

Samantha swam back to the wall and Nikki dove into the pool doing breaststroke. "WHAT THE HELL ARE YOU DUMBASSES DOING?! HURRY UP SO WE CAN BEAT THESE WIMPS!" Emily screamed at her team. Coach Mandy blew her whistle at Emily from the bleachers. "Emily, language. Show some positivity and encouragement toward your teammates." "Ugh, fine."

The rest of the freestyle swimmers swam back to the wall and the breaststroke swimmers jumped into the pool.

Nikki was swimming very slow when she saw other swimmers being ahead of her. She was starting to doubt herself until she heard her teammates and her group cheering her on. "GO NIKKI! GO! YOU CAN DO THIS!" Nikki swam past the swimmers that were above her and she flip-turned back to the starting line. "GO NIKKI!" Wren cheered, standing on the starting block. "If you start before me or beat me, you're going to regret joining this team," Emily threatened Wren, also standing on the starting block. "Whatever, I don't care if I win or lose. Just as long as I'm having fun. And I believe you should feel the same for yourself and your team," Wren politely responded, giving Emily a big smile. Emily shook her head and looked at her own lane. *Why is this girl so positive? Why...is...she so special?*

Nikki swam back to the wall and Wren jumped into the pool, doing the butterfly stroke. *What the? She started without me. This bi-* One of Emily's teammates stopped at the wall and Emily jumped into the pool, doing butterfly too. "You're not gonna get away with this, Wren," she yelled. "Let's see about that," Wren said and she swam ahead of Emily and flip-turned back to the starting wall. "No. Wait," Emily complained as she saw Wren swimming back to the starting lane. She also flip-turned and followed Wren to the starting wall. "You won't beat me, Wren. When I win, you and your group will bow down before me and my teammates." Wren ignored her and swam ahead of Emily again. Emily gasped and tried catching up to her, but by the time Emily caught up, Wren got out of the pool. "The Swordfish team won round one," said the announcer, through the microphone and speakers. The audience cheered and so did Wren's family. "THAT'S OUR DAUGHTER!" Mr. and Mrs.Sky screamed, hugging Mikayla tightly.

"You're…crushing…me," Mikayla complained, trying to breathe through their hug.

Emily got out of the pool and felt defeated. "I-I-I-I lost. H-h-h-how did this happen? I was so close to her." Coach Mandy slowly walked behind Emily, patting her right shoulder. "There, there, Emily. We'll get them during the next round. Just sit down, okay?" she kindly said, walking Emily to the bleachers. *But I won't be in the next round.*

Meanwhile, Wren, Samantha, Bianca, and Nikki were sitting on the bleachers, cheering about their win. "WE WON! WE WON! WE WON!" "I'm so proud of us," Samantha said, squeezing Wren's hands. "I know. I feel like we're superheroes who defeated our first bad guys," Wren said. "You mean like magical girls?" Bianca smiled and they all continued to cheer except for Nikki.

After Nikki saw the competition between Wren and Emily, she felt scared because since Wren defeated Emily, she was afraid that Wren would get hurt like her old friend, Sarah from swim camp. "Wren?" she called, gently tapping her left shoulder. "Now that you defeated Emily, aren't you scared that she's gonna ask for a rematch or hurt you?" Wren looked at the ceiling, thinking about Emily's words from the locker room. "Nah, not really. Like I said, I'm ready for whatever happens to me. At least I won my first competition," Wren shrugged. "Okay. just be careful," Nikki gulped.

During the last two rounds of the swim meet, the Swordfish and the Sharks were doing another set, a relay race and an individual race.

At the end of the swim meet, few of the swimmers got their medals. Wren, Samantha, Bianca, and Nikki all won first place. Few of the Swordfish team were placed in first and second. Emily and her relay group were placed in fourth place while most of her team were placed in second and third place. "At least we tried our best," Coach Mandy smiled, patting Emily's head. "This can't be happening. This can't be real," Emily muttered. "I got defeated by a newbie. I was supposed to win. Not Wren. This battle can not be over yet."

The announcer congratulated the swimmers and announced the winner of the swim meet. "The winner of this swim meet is…THE SWORDFISH TEAM!" The crowd went wild and the whole team hugged each other. Coach Nelly was crying tears of joy. "MY BABIES!" She screamed. The announcer wished the Sharks team the best of luck for next time's swim meet, and thanked the audience for coming to the swim meet.

As soon as the audience was about to pack their stuff and the swimmers were walking towards the locker room, Emily ran to a white table that's in front of the white board, grabbed an extra microphone off the table and screamed, "WREN SKY! I CHALLENGE YOU TO REMATCH!"

10

The audience and the swimmers were silent. Samantha, Bianca, and Nikki gulped. "Oh no," Nikki whispered. "Excuse me?" Wren questioned. "WREN SKY! I CHALLENGE YOU TO REMATCH!" Emily desperately repeated. "What kind of rematch?" Coach Nelly angrily stepped in. "100 yd butterfly. Wren vs Emily," she replied.

Mr. and Mrs.Sky and Mikayla felt scared and Coach Nelly and the team looked at Wren, feeling anxious. "Wren, you don't have to do the rematch. You won. You can go home and rest your body," Coach Nelly begged. "Please, Wren don't do this. We don't want you to get hurt like Sarah. Just go home and rest," Nikki loudly cried, hugging Wren by her legs. "I accept your challenge," Wren confidently said, walking towards Emily. "Are you sure if this is what you want?" Emily sassily asked through the microphone. Wren frustratedly snatched the microphone out of Emily's hand and gave her the death glare. "Yes, I'm sure. Let's get this over with because I have a family who needs me to be home right now to celebrate. And if I win, don't even try to harm me like you harmed Sarah back at swim camp." The audience, the swimmers, the coaches, Wren's parents, and Mikayla gasped. "WHAT HAPPENED TO SARAH?!" Mikayla worriedly yelled. "IS SHE ALIVE?! IF YOU'RE PLANNING TO KILL MY BIG SISTER WE'RE GONNA HAVE A FREAKIN PROBLEM!" Emily snatched the microphone back and screamed at Mikayla. "SHUT THE FUCK UP YOU STARVING ARTIST! NOBODY'S TALKING TO YOU!" Wren looked shocked after hearing Emily name-calling her baby sister in front of everybody. She snatched the microphone out of Emily's hand again. "HEY SORE LOSER, THAT'S MY TWIN SISTER YOU'RE TALKING TO YOU. TAKE A JAB AT MY SISTER ONE MORE TIME OR THAT'S GOING TO BE YOUR LAST SENTENCE TONIGHT!" And shoved the microphone back at Emily's chest and stood behind the starting block. "Are we going to do this or what?"

Emily put the microphone close to her mouth and replied, "Let's go, bookworm." And her and Wren stood on the starting blocks. The announcer shrugged his shoulders and announced the rematch. "Ladies and gentlemen, before you all can go home, we're going to do a rematch. Emily vs Wren. Tonight's rematch will be an individual 100 yd butterfly race. Winner gets to take home a golden medal."

During the announcement, Emily and Wren were whispering to each other. "I don't care if you're in the advanced stage, I'm still going to kick your ass," Emily threatened. Wren shook her head. "You know, threatening me and other people will get you hurt. If you keep that up, you won't be able to have friends."

The announcer started the countdown, "You girls ready? On your mark. Get set. GO!" Wren and Emily dove into the water, and started doing the butterfly stroke. Both of their teams and Wren's family started cheering them on.

Emily was ahead of Wren until Wren moved ahead of her where she did a flip-turn and swam back to the starting lane. *I'm not gonna let her win.* Emily said in her head as soon as she saw Wren swimming to another direction in the pool. Emily then touched the wall and flip-turned back to the starting lane, but by the time she did that, Wren was already flip-turning to the other side of the pool once again. Emily began to slow down.

The audience was so amazed at Wren's speed, they all cheered for Wren more than Emily. "GO SPEED-GIRL! GO SPEED-GIRL!" "There goes our Sonic The Hedgehog," Mr.Sky commented. Bianca heard Mr.Sky's comment and told Samantha and Nikki. "Girls, did you hear what Mr.Sky said? He called Wren 'Sonic The Hedgehog.' Maybe that can be her nickname for our team." "Great idea, let me tell the others," Samantha agreed and whispered the nickname idea to the team and Coach Nelly. Coach Nelly was the last person Samantha told it to and she excitedly nodded her head and they all screamed, "GOTTA GO FAST, SONIC! KICK HER ASS!" "Who the hell is Sonic?" Emily muttered in the water. "They're probably referring to me," Wren happily answered, did a flip-turn and dashed through the water, swimming back to the other direction again to end the rematch. "NO! NO! YOU CAN'T WIN AGAIN! YOU'RE A NEWBIE!" Emily cried. "SHARKS! SAY SOMETHING TO ENCOURAGE ME!"

The Sharks were about to encourage Emily to keep going, but they had a flashback of her calling one of the teammates a 'dumbass' during round one. To hit Emily with karma, they crossed their arms and shook their heads. "Say something, please?" she begged, but still no answer.

By the time Emily begged her team to encourage her, Wren got out of the pool and cheered with her arms up in the air yelling, "I WON! I WON!" Emily quickly flip-turned back to the starting lane and butterflied all the way down until she reached the wall. She got out of the pool and the announcer revealed the winner. "The winner of the rematch is Wren Sky." And everybody applauded. Including The Sharks.

Coach Nelly grabbed a gold medal off a black table and wrapped it around Wren's neck. "Wren won the rematch," she cheered and so did everybody else.

Emily got out of the pool and yelled at her team for not cheering her on. "I HATE YOU GUYS! YOU GUYS ARE TRAITORS!" Mikayla ran down the bleacher stairs and wrapped Wren around with a blue towel and gave her a big hug. "You're a hero, sis. I'm proud of you. Thank you for standing up for me." Wren smiled with tears in her eyes and hugged Mikayla back. "Aw, thank you. Are your feelings hurt?" "Not really. I just shrugged it off."

Emily walked towards Wren and pointed at her with her index finger. "I want another rematch?" "Another one?" Everybody said. "Weren't you just defeated twice?" Mikayla reminded her. "Yeah, and we all are tired and hungry," Bianca joined in. "How about next time?" Wren suggested and walked to the locker room to change into her casual clothes. The rest of the swimmers followed her while shoving Emily out of the way.

Emily stood there, looking at Wren walking into the locker room, feeling defeated and despair. Coach Mandy stood next to her, wrapping her arm around her shoulders. "Don't be mad, Emily. There's always next time." Emily looked at Coach Mandy with red glowing eyes. "Why didn't you guys cheer for me?" "Because you called one of your teammates a 'dumbass' and that was so uncalled for. Maybe if you respect your teammates, we would have encouraged you," Coach Mandy fought back. "I was only trying to help." Coach Mandy face palmed and pushed Emily towards the locker room door. "Go change or else I will suspend you for cursing at your teammates." Emily peeked through the locker room door, staring at Wren, feeling jealous. "This isn't over yet," she muttered, "This won't be our last rematch."

TO BE CONTINUED...

ABOUT THE AUTHOR

Mya "JournalismCat" Jackson is a young self-publish author who lives in Michigan with a loving mother and father and an older brother and twin sister. She was born with a speech impediment where she stutters. Her favorite hobbies are swimming, writing, reading, gaming, and singing. And she is the author behind her first book "One Helluva Friday."

CHECK OUT JOURNALISMCAT'S

FIRST BOOK

TGIF! The five cousins are out of school for the weekend. They have plans for their own Friday night. Lucy and Amy are going to a party. Tori, Lara, and Khloe are staying at home chilling. Tori, Lara, and Khloe don't get along so well. Neither does Roland and Amy. Tori and Lara think Khloe is annoying and too young to hang out with and Roland doesn't allow Amy to leave the house and party with her friend, Jade. Let's see how they are on Friday night.